Mama's Gloves

To Mom, who is always there no matter where she is
—Mike Huber

To my beautiful wife, Kari, whose undying support makes everything possible
—Joseph Cowman

Published by Redleaf Lane
An imprint of Redleaf Press
10 Yorkton Court
Saint Paul, MN 55117
www.RedleafLane.org

First edition 2014
Book jacket and interior page design by Jim Handrigan
Main body text set in Billy
Typeface provided by MyFonts

Manufactured in Canada
20 19 18 17 16 15 14 13   1 2 3 4 5 6 7 8

Library of Congress Control Number: 2013939325

Mama's Gloves

Written by
MIKE HUBER

Illustrated by
JOSEPH COWMAN

Redleaf
Lane

Another morning at child care.

As he arrived, Esteban smiled at his teacher, Walter, and Walter smiled back.

Walter always waited to talk to Esteban until Esteban and his mama had read a book together.

When they finished reading,
Mama Lucia gave Esteban
two kisses and a hug,
mwah-mwah-mmmm.
Then she left.

Esteban and Walter went to
the window to wave good-bye.
Esteban waved until Mama
Lucia was out of sight.
Then he turned around.
He couldn't believe it!

Mama Lucia's gloves were lying on the floor next to the reading chair,

one drooped over the other.

Esteban turned back to the window.
"Mama!"

Walter said, "It can be hard to say good-bye to your mama.
You know she always comes back at the end of the day."

Esteban ran to the gloves and held them up. "But she left her gloves! Her hands will get cold!"

"Oh dear," said Walter. "We better send her a note so she won't worry. What should we say?"

Esteban held the gloves close. He said, "You forgot your gloves. I'll make sure they're safe. You will see them at the end of the day. That's when you pick me up."

Esteban went to his cubby and unzipped the special pocket on his backpack. It smelled like the frijoles and cilantro his grandmother made. He put the gloves next to the photo of his family. They would be safe there.

But he still felt sad. He went to the art table to draw a picture.

He used lots of green. Green was his favorite color.
He drew red flowers. Mama Lucia loved red flowers.

He drew his family. He finished it with a sun up above.

Esteban felt sunnier inside when he looked at his picture.

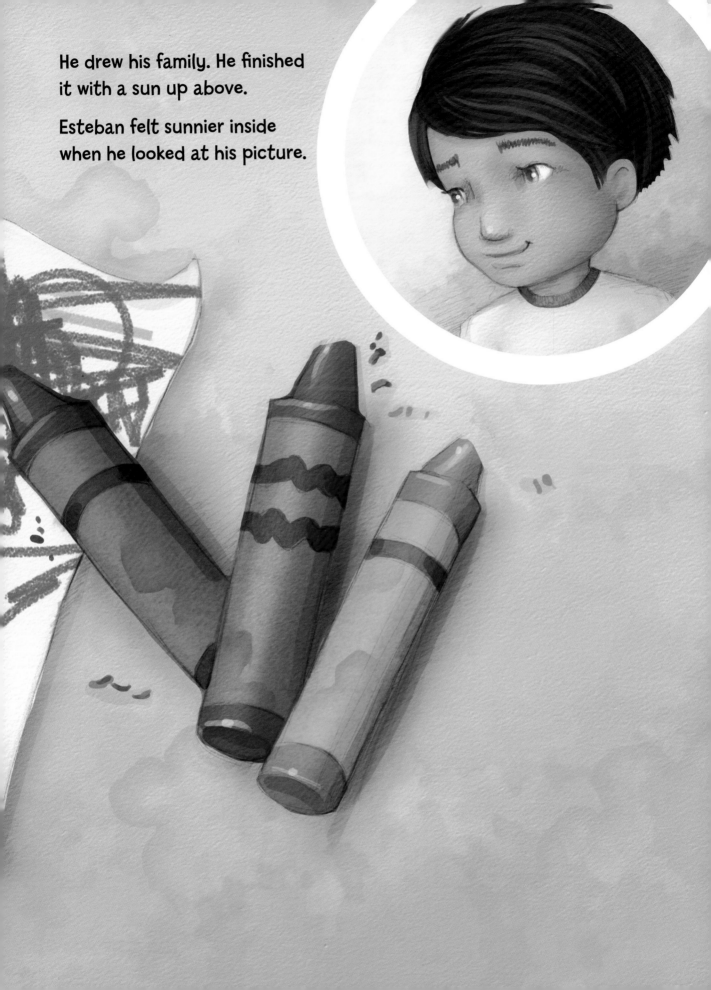

At naptime, Esteban went to his cubby to get Perrito. As he unzipped his backpack, he remembered the gloves. He would take those too.

Walter sat by Esteban. "Mama Lucia is lucky she has you to take such good care of her gloves."

Esteban gave the gloves two kisses and a hug,
mwah-mwah-mmmm.

Soon he fell asleep.

After naptime, Esteban launched his spaceship from the saving shelf and zoomed around Padma and the barn.

A few orbits later, Esteban wondered if the gloves were still safe. He asked Padma, "Can I park my spaceship next to your barn?"

"Okay," said Padma.

Esteban checked his backpack. Mama's gloves were still where he put them, snug against Perrito. They were safe, so he could keep playing.

He walked back to Padma. "Do any of your animals want a ride on my spaceship?"

"Bye-bye, piggy," Padma said.

Esteban and Padma were still playing with the farm when Esteban saw Mama Lucia walk by the window. It was already the end of the day!

He ran to his backpack and grabbed the gloves.

When Mama walked in, Esteban jumped up and down and held her gloves high.

"Look!" he said. "They're still safe!"

"My hands were cold, but I knew you would warm them up,"
Mama Lucia said. She smiled and gave Esteban two kisses and a hug,
mwah-mwah-mmmm.

"Chiquito, I'm always a little warmer when I pick you up."

A Note to Readers

Sometimes Esteban gets upset because he misses his mama after she drops him off at child care. It's not unusual for young children to struggle when it's time to say good-bye to a loved one, but that doesn't make separating or being apart any easier. Adults often struggle too—parents, as they try to find just the right way to say good-bye, and caregivers, as they try to provide comfort.

You can help children through this significant transition by establishing a consistent and upbeat drop-off routine— like the way Mama Lucia reads to Esteban and gives him two kisses and a hug before Walter comes over. You can acknowledge the emotions of a child who is upset and provide reassurance. Walter does this when he tells Esteban, "It can be hard to say good-bye to your mama. You know she always comes back at the end of the day." And the child benefits when you—parents and caregivers—communicate about how the child is doing throughout the day.

We hope *Mama's Gloves* assures children that even when it's hard to say good-bye to a loved one, another caring adult is always nearby, and a reunion with family at the end of the day is a sure thing.